I0626622

Erenarch Academy:
UNDER THE DRAGON BANNER

Dragon Stead Series Book 1

JULIANA REW

Cover Art by Keely Rew

Erenarch Academy: Under the Dragon Banner

By Juliana Rew

Copyright 2018 Juliana Rew
ISBN -13:978-1-7322189-0-1

Discover other titles by Juliana Rew:

Miranda of Daris
Daris Moon
Mountain Ma'am
The Adventures of Mountain Ma'am

License Notes

Cover: Keely Rew

www.julianarew.com

Dedication

For Russ and Keely, who helped bring Dragon Stead into being.

*****~~~~~*****

Contents

*****~~~~~****

Chapter One

The Birth of a Dragon

When I first began teaching at Erenarch Academy, I felt honored to be chosen to begin the tutelage of civilization's finest young minds. Looking back, I realize my naiveté in believing that residing on Erenarch exempted us from the ravages of events, even at interplanetary distances. Sometimes my heart is heavy when I recall my role in preparing students to endure untold hardships in order to ensure our survival. Though I should have known better, I was guilty of discouraging or minimizing the affection my students had for one another, dismissing it as "puppy love." Other times I felt gratitude and pride in their accomplishments. This is our chronicle.

***

For the past half a millennium, what began a "space race" had slowed to a creep as ou ancestors discovered how hard it was to mov beyond Earth's solar system. We couldn't travel faster than light, and the distance to the next star was measured in light-years. We couldn't communicate faster than light, so even if we did reach a distant star, those back on Earth would be long dead. Space, radiation, and dust all conspired to kill us. We stubbornly persisted, however, eking out small victories against the universe's plan to keep us in our place.

Forty years ago, I was fresh from university on Iles de Saintes within the planetary system of Sigma Draconis, 18.8 light-years from Earth. Take that, universe.

I had traveled for three months, interspersed with periods of cold sleep, to reach Erenarch Academy to assume an assistant professorship at the premier vocational college for the future leaders of the system popularly known as Dragon Stead. Perhaps the dragon symbol that was to become our class mascot hung about in my subconscious even then.

A language teacher, my subject was not considered one of the most important at Erenarch, but the Academy agreed that a broad education was the best preparation for leadership.

I myself was not leadership material, except in the didactic sense, but I was a chap who found dozens of fields to be equally fascinating. One of my college professors called it the "Renaissance syndrome." I, of course, had no objection to being compared with artist-scientists on ancient Earth such as Leonardo da Vinci. My job would be to provide a little fatherly guidance and help the children discover their intellectual passions.

The Birth of a Dragon

I piled my bags just inside the arch entrance of the Administration Building. As I entered, the disembodied voice of the campus computer greeted me softly. "Welcome, Dr. Creev Proceed to the rear wall to meet Dr. Gray." I resiste the urge to turn around and around slowly, tryir hard to keep my mouth from falling open. Th lobby of Admin was impressively large, and aliv with holographic images of the famous graduates the academy. Scattered among them were silve suited administrator holos, one of whom saunter up to point me in the right direction.

"Will there be other new faculty arriving?" asked, not knowing whether to speak to the air or the image before me.

"Yes, Dr. Gray is expecting you and tw others," the administrator replied.

He gestured toward a spot on the floor, anc took a step toward it. Suddenly I felt a floatir sensation, which at first I thought was anticipator but turned out to be a sliding cushion of air, know as an antigrav assist. A breeze riffled my red hair, which I was quite proud and wore long, in the sty of the day.

The antigrav deposited me gently near large expanse of featureless white wall. surreptitiously tried to adjust my sash, which w decorated with a row of Celtic knots and tl rampant stag of my alma mater, Tarant University

"By the way," the administrator said. "We be getting you an Academy robe, so you won't hav to wear that embarrassing college getup." That w my first inkling that perhaps the world of bagpip and reels might not be considered the highest sta of civilization in the solar system.

I muttered a few choice imprecations in ancient Welsh and hoped the computer translated for whoever guided the administrator's tongue.

"Ahem; well yes, sorry about that," said a very real-looking young fellow, who turned out to be Donal Gray, my department chairman and best friend for the next several decades. "It's a pleasure to meet you, Rowan," he said. "Please call me Donal."

Donal was a fine example of the peacekeeping branch of humanity. He rarely raised his voice to anyone, whereas I rarely missed such an opportunity. His dark hair curled gently around his face, which I can only describe as cherubic. I fingered my shillelagh speculatively. The nasty little stunners on the current shillelagh made them effective, if risky, teaching tools. Donal's sweet smile convinced me he didn't really need a lesson that day.

We marched toward his office, collecting another young recruit along the way; Hilly Gerhart. Like Donal, he came from the planet Sharra, renowned for their computer and AI expertise. (Hilly didn't last long as a teacher, but that's another story.)

Donal dismissed the administrator and invited Hilly and me to have a seat. A tall brunette already sat in one of Donal's leather chairs, swinging a well-turned ankle above crossed legs. She was introduced as Miranda Powers, a second-year teacher who would help show me the ropes. She shook our hands with a powerful grip. Miranda was a martial arts and survival expert, and I didn't doubt for a moment that she could easily best us all. Miranda regaled us with some of her previous

exploits in a few of the more barbarous systems c
the Draconis rim. Like my father, she was a vetera
of off-planet wars.

Miranda had a good laugh at my person
stunner.

"Those can be useful for stirring martinis
she snickered. But truth be told, how often would
be called upon to shred enemies with devastatir
antipersonnel weapons? So far, never.

I was a lover, not a fighter.

Hilly was a mathematician, and seemed
retreat behind an imaginary curtain of thought.

He sat, blinking occasionally when Mirano
punctuated one of her phrases in a particular
explosive way. He did seem to warm up slight
when Donal would ask him an esoteric ma
question. Hilly later told me he didn't have muc
use for people socially, but he did respect Dona
competence.

I myself did have use for people. I rememb
standing out on the boulevard in front of n
parents' flat on Tarant at the age of three, sayir
"hello" to every adult who went by until they a
said "hello" back. If "hello" didn't work, I trie
"bonjour," "bore da," or "dia dhuit." By the time
was twelve, I was ready to say it in Ipili, Kashmi
and Kickapoo. Anything to get a "hi," that was m
It was difficult for me to accept that people lil
Hilly didn't need friends at work, only colleague
The best I could do over time was to launch a volle
of jovial greetings his way and scurry away befo
an uncomfortable silence ensued.

As the get-acquainted conversation wane
Donal offered to escort us to the student cente
where our nostrils were assailed with the welcon

smell of meat pasties. I chose one, which was vacuumed up by the kitchen bot and delivered to me in a shiny thermal bag. Students had made meat pasties their staple at Erenarch because they could be eaten without utensils, usually while the student was running from one class to another. Pasties also held up well under all sorts of classroom conditions, such as complete darkness or weightlessness. The main trick was to smuggle them past the teachers. I had nothing against them as long as the students didn't use them as missiles.

Whereas the administration building had been a dazzling hall of flashing monitors, comm screens, and holograms, the student union was dark, lit by a few shafts of sunlight, pools of light illuminating some food or beverage bar, and a teeming mass of noisy young people. They sat on soft pillows, chattering to friends, studying (it seemed), or managing to guide food to their mouths while staring at a book. Some were tapping words into their books or exercising their virtual pets. There was a "no pets" policy at Erenarch, but if the pet was an AI, it was viewed as a possible aide for the student.

Our student center was much like any other, but I knew that most of these students had spent their entire childhoods at Erenarch after having been chosen to be levitated to the position of Future Great Leader. A few had never seen their parents, having been genetically designed and produced. The youngest were barely out of primary school, and the teachers and the older students were the substitute parents here. We were "in loco parentis," but also "in loco planetas." No longer citizens of their home planets, these were future operatives the Erenarch Network, even if they were just kids.

I remembered my life before I went college. My parents traveled with me to visit tl university on Tarant a year in advance, glued opposite sides of me for the campus tour. The were at once trying to decide if this place was goc enough for their precious offspring, and trying cope with the idea of letting me loose into the va Dragon Stead.

My father was a Corps master helmsma and looked invincible in his uniform. He had nev been to college but was a decorated veteran of tl Intersystem War, and this entitled members of h family to paid educations. He had spent so muc time on battle cruisers that he seemed out of pla in the benign, landscaped grounds of the universit

My mother clutched the catalog, ready fight on my behalf if anyone should question m right to be at this college. I blushed a little as the snapped holos of me in front of every possible iv covered building. I stole glances at the oth students while pretending my parents werer standing in plain sight for all to see. We spent tl next year preparing for my departure to the halls academe. When I got there at last, I relished tl glorious freedom.

The parents of the children at Erenarch d not come for tours, or even for visits. It was not th they didn't love their children: it was just that the children now had a new home. Some of them mig return someday to lead their home planets, or the might never be heard from again. Either way, it w a great honor.

Military regalia were in evidence, varying from modern Corps fatigues to ancient swords and stunners, at least on the part of the teachers. A demo of single combat unfolded on the small raised stage in the student union. Blaring music accompanied the melee, while a student shouted a squeaky blow-by-blow commentary into a microphone. Donal and Miranda described with pride the martial arts training at Erenarch Academy, which culminated in weekly strategic battles. Students were assigned to teams, given practice resources and weapons, and expected to compete that Saturday. Part of the following week was given to dissecting the battle, what went wrong, who did what to whom, and so forth.

I didn't have much interest in battle, and said so to Donal. Not that I hadn't learned some self-defense skills, but on my planet people tended to use technological solutions, like protective force fields or invisibility cloaks. My instincts were more likely to cause me to shift to a shape that was congruent to the situation...no need to battle if it wasn't necessary, after all.

"Maybe you should be a coach," he replied. That's how I got the assignment of being a coach for my class in the next competition. This would include designing a banner to be carried by the team. This sounded more like being a cheerleader than a coach to me, but I allowed as how I ought to be able to research the medieval coats of arms and come up with a suitable symbol.

Donal informed us our bags had been taken to our quarters in the faculty apartments.

I had a shipment of furniture and favorite paper books coming soon, although Erenarch had

the largest library in the known nebula, and
course everyone was under the watchful eyes of tl
Dragon Stead Network.

*****~~~~~*****

Chapter Two

First Day of School

A few days after my arrival at Erenarc Academy, my classes began. I had a bit of time settle in. My quarters were small, but they we equipped with vidwalls where we could create virtual panorama and avoid claustrophobia. I ha set the vidwalls with a grassy meadow sheltered t sheer red cliffs. After admiring the scenery, I shoc out my professor's robe and laid it on the bed.

Metallic embroidery traced the Erenarch log on the breast, glinting in the ruddy light. I avoide dressing for as long as possible, putting in a quic twenty-minute running workout. When I fanciful imagined that the cliffs looked marginally closer, staggered off the mat and ducked into the son shower. Dressing, I pulled on the unitard and rob and pinned on a symbol from my home plan Tarant; a rampant bird above a triskelion with blue sapphire center. Finally, I ran my finge through my hair, and after practicing a ster professorial glower in the mirror, I stepped out into a crisp fall morning.

Erenarch Academy, like most well funded institutions of higher learning, tried to emulate the look of ancient historical universities dating back to Earth's middle ages. Although many thought of universities as frivolous "ivory towers" unconnected to reality, I for one appreciated the connection to the past. As the saying went, "those who do not remember the past are doomed to repeat it."

Arriving at the quadrangle, I could see students streaming in all directions toward their first class. A few small pods materialized and disgorged passengers, but most of the students were too young to drive except in simulations or during training courses. The Language Arts building was at one corner, a squat Gothic-style castle of natural sedimentary stone. My room was open, and several young students were already sitting at their benches.

The room setup included rows of single benches extending across the width of the room. Each child had a vidbook for taking notes. The vidbooks were the students' connection to the Network, and could be used in voice mode or keyboard mode. The children appeared to range in age from six to twelve. I was a bit surprised that they weren't segregated by age, but all of these kids were certified geniuses and could probably hold their own with older classmates, at least intellectually. Some of the children were young enough that they still were using the keyboard until they could master the fine-motor skills necessary for writing cursive.

First Day of School

I walked to my podium, keyed in m
passphrase, and projected a holograph
blackboard.

These holoboards served as the main tool
our trade. If you suspected your charges of n
paying sufficient attention, you could step throug
the board and turn around to face the class. Th
required skill in writing backwards, but it w.
worth the effort to acquire the ability just to enjc
seeing the expressions on the students' faces tl
first time they saw it done. I could manipulate tl
board with hand signals and provide notes th
would write themselves in the students' book
Holo projections helped me show dialogues
species speaking the language of the week, or nev
broadcasts from across the galactic quadrant. I ofte
showed dramatizations originating on oth
worlds, since I felt these gave both a flavor for tl
language and for the hopes and fantasies of tl
peoples (and species) inhabiting these world
Besides, living in a rather sheltered academic wor.
my whole life made me hungry to experience lif
albeit vicariously. And who better to discu
current events with than eager, impressionab
young minds?

When I started teaching at Erenarch for
years ago, we endeavored to give students tl
ability to speak around two hundred languages l
the time they left the Academy. (Of course, tod*a*
there are many more important languages, b
having this small base and a knowledge of the roo
of many important languages helps our form
students get by in an off-world encounter.)

Languages proliferated on every inhabite
planet, new ones springing up, old languag

morphing, sometimes in a very short time. So we had a need to keep up with languages of known species, as well as to be able to communicate almost immediately when encountering newsents, newly sentient species or beings. Most of what we considered new species had their origins on old Earth but had risen to sentience. AIs did most of the work of stripping down new languages, and determining their grammar, syntax, and vocabulary. Most civilized species in Dragon Stead had mastered broadcasting, so we could usually get up to speed quickly on idioms and slang. This was still where our students were important, however, since misunderstandings were all too common, even among native language speakers.

As I gazed out at my first class, I was not yet plagued by fears of an age gap between children and professors (as I certainly am today.) So I decided to start with an old tale with a strong father figure. It was in Germanic, called "Das Ring der Nibelung." We downloaded Germanic into our brains and began to explore the story. The tale of swords, sorcery, the sleeping maiden surrounded by a ring of fire, and a fire-breathing dragon guarding a hoard of gold, all were guaranteed to capture the imaginations of young listeners. (The tale fascinates me to this day because the motivations are so complex.) How would I act if I were the top god of the universe, forced to deal with unruly relatives and jealous enemies?

***

Wotan, the father god, seemed to let miscreants like Loge and Mime get away with theft and murder, while he tried to act like he was above

it all by stealing a dwarf's hoard of gold to pay f
the building of Valhalla, the new home of the gods

***

I asked the class, "Does Wotan's behavi
seem out of bounds?" One of the students, Adamn
Anabalegu, said, "I think since he's the king, l
should be able to do what he thinks is best." I lat
learned that Adamma had been a princess on h
home planet.

***

The hoard included a magical gold ring, ar
the dwarf cursed Wotan for taking it. The cur:
threatened to bring the rule of the gods to an en
so Wotan embarked on a series of quests to see if l
could avert this fate. He went to talk to Erde, tl
Norn who had foretold his doom. He ended ι
fathering eight warrior daughters by Erde, know
as the Valkyrie, including the beautiful Brunnhilde

***

"Has anyone heard of the Norns?" I asked tl
class. I explained that the Erenarch Network
supercomputer, the most powerful in the syster
had been nicknamed "the Norns." So this German
tale had inspired the name of the AI that tl
Network used to predict and steer Network affairs

***

Getting back to the story, we read that Wota
had also fathered a human hero, Sigmund, wl
could win back the ring that would save the worl
Wotan gave Sigmund a magic helmet and swor

Sigmund fell in love with a woman who, unbeknownst to him, was his twin sister.

***

"Isn't that a problem, marrying your sister?" asked a tiny little boy about six years old.

The roster said he was Declan Ryan.

"Well, Declan, yes, that sort of behavior was considered immoral in that culture, and it could lead to genetic defects in offspring."

I hadn't calculated on having to explain the facts of life to my students, but we made a small digression to bring everyone up to speed. Young Declan might not have a chance to use this knowledge right away, but at least he would be prepared.

***

In one of the more wrenching passages of the story, Wotan confided his plight to Brunnhilde, saying he treasured love above all, but he was forced to eschew it and abandon the plan to win the ring. Poor Brunnhilde tried to help him by disregarding his orders to kill the hero. Wotan was so enraged he killed Sigmund himself and got rid of Brunnhilde, the one person who reflected his true soul. It was hard to understand how a loving father could kill his own son and take away his daughter's "godhood," banishing her to die.

Wotan gave all the gold, including the ring, to the builder of Valhalla, Fafner the giant. Fafner promptly turned into a ferocious fire-breathing dragon to better guard the ring among his hoard of gold.

As expected, my young students liked tł
dragon best, and the hero Siegfried, Sigmunc
orphaned son.

***

Siegfried grew up in the forest, raised by tł
brother of the dwarf, and was handed the helm
and sword with a suggestion to kill the dragon. ł
was young, brash, and up to the task.

***

"Does anyone see any common them(
between dragon-slaying and today's world?"
asked.

A deafening silence.

I looked down the student roster. "Ashley?"

Ashley Emerson turned out to be
prepubescent girl with blue-highlighted haî
multiple piercings, and all-black clothing, wh
there was of it. I later learned that the piercinȝ
were all AI implants, and that Ashley was the st
programmer of the Academy. Ashley coyly avoide
the question by bringing up a holo of the Drac
nebula and pointing out that Erenarch is at the edȝ
of the Sigma Draconis system.

"That's a very good observation, Ashley. In
way, Draconis system is like a large dragon that v
are constantly trying to tame."

I patted myself on the back that I hâ
successfully managed to invoke a metaphor on tł
first day of class. Feeling I was on a roll, I sudden
remembered my assignment of designing a cla
banner.

"What would you all think of choosing a dragon as our class mascot?" I asked.

I rather pushed the idea, since the red dragon of Cymru was also the mascot of my Welsh forebears on my home planet of Tarant in Iles des Saintes quadrant.

The dragon banner would become the symbol around which many a future team would coalesce. When students matured enough to outgrow the banner, I devoutly hoped the concept of team spirit would persist in their little psyches. Erenarch was not strictly a military academy, but the mock battles my students would fight and the stratagems they developed would serve them well when Erenarch expanded to encompass more of Dragon Stead and its nearby star systems.

*****~~~~~*****

Chapter Three

Pitched Battle

The week after we chose our dragon mascot assigned reports to the students that I thoug would provide character-building learnir experiences, such as the destruction of tl Delphinia or the discovery of the planet Dari Although there was some groaning at havir homework already, I deflected this with news of tl first intramural battle competition.

"We are going to be a team at the fir competition in two weeks, and we could use up six volunteers to be in single combat," I said. On four hands went up.

"Anybody else?" Nothing.

I consulted my roster, hovering in the far le of my field of vision.

"Parsons. Rick, is there any way you cou participate? Have you had any experience wi weapons?"

Parsons looked down. He was one of tl older students in class, around twelve, perhaps.

"I was in it last term, but I got my butt kicked," he said. I later learned that he got his butt kicked every day the previous term.

"Maybe we could get some extra coaching from the martial arts instructor, Miss Powers," I suggested.

"Her team was unbeatable last term. None of the rest of us had a chance," Rick noted.

I made a note to myself to talk with Miranda. I mostly wanted our team to do their best even if they got defeated, but I also hoped she could help us identify a "natural" who could be the team's leader/hero.

"Class is dismissed. Rick, if you are willing, I'd like you to join the other four and give it the old college try." Rick grudgingly assented, and the students bolted for the door.

One girl, Adamma, lingered behind,. Adamma was a pretty, chubby black child who had an extravagantly happy demeanor. At first impression, I wouldn't have taken her seriously. But then I saw she had a black panther AI that her father, a king back on Nioba, had sent with her to the Academy. He sat down beside Adamma and regarded me coolly with phosphorescent green eyes.

Adamma said, "Dr. Creeve, I'd like to be on the team, but I can't fight. My panther, Serrahji, has always done all my fighting for me. Perhaps I could be the team manager."

I sighed. A challenge we faced as teachers at Erenarch Academy was that all of our students were classified as natural leaders. This made teamwork a challenge. I foresaw that we would be strong on ideas and strategy, but weaker on follow-through. The goal would be to give the team tl strength to do what needed to be done; a tall ord when they would be getting beaten down k fellows who were physically stronger than the were. We were pretty feckless in the batt department.

I agreed that Adamma would be our tea manager, although at the time I was stymied as what she might usefully do.

I headed for lunch at the student unio remembering to pick up a mango smoothie, whic I'd gotten hooked on at Tarant. I admired the wa the campus was housed in a fall scene with gree grass and gold- and red-leaved trees. The clima control was programmed to mimic the seasons Earth's temperate zone. Erenarch's natural clima was a bit on the chilly side, at minus fifty degree Celsius. It was possible to go outside tl settlements, but you had to wear a heatsuit to kee warm and protect against the rugged terrain.

I didn't see Miranda in the student union, s after I finished my smoothie, I walked toward tl stadium, where her office was located. She wasr there, so I wandered by the gym, where I saw number of students working out, some fightir holos of humans and creatures. Across the room spotted Miranda.

"Keep your guard up, dummy," she shoute "It's better to get hit in the arm than the head, get i Then hit 'em back with the other arm!"

I zigzagged over to her. "Miranda, may I hav a word?"

"Sure, what's up?"

I told her about the Dragon team and ho our fuzzy-brained bunch of intellectuals wo doomed to repeat history if we didn't get some help quickly. I also mentioned the bullying that had occurred last term.

"Why don't you all just turn into a bunch of mice and scurry off?" she joked, knowing that was how we Celts tended to cope.

"Well, not all my students are mice or men," I retorted. "Some are girls." That shut her up…temporarily.

The next day at the end of class I announced a practice schedule. "We'll be doing a half hour during lunch and an hour after dinner," I noted. "Miss Powers has kindly consented to letting you work with her team." A chorus of moans ensued. "Just think of this as a great opportunity," I said.

"A great opportunity to get massacred," Ashley cracked. Ashley already had a great grasp of the concept of irony, but I hoped she would also learn how to rise to the occasion.

We all trouped out to grab some nourishment at the student union before flying over to the stadium.

"This is where we will do the competition," I said. "The holos will be adjusted to look like a battlefield with armies on both sides. Of course, there will just be our little squads fighting in the middle at the front of their minions." The kids laughed, and we walked over to the gym.

Our team consisted of Rick, Ashley, Edward, Andrew, and Declan. Declan was the youngest, and still just a puny little featherweight. He had a heck of a kick, though, and could give you a thorough tongue-lashing with his comically salty vocabulary, which some might characterize as "colorful." It appeared that somewhere along the way he ha picked up extensive training in strategic swearing.

Andrew was the senior of the group, alreac a teen. He had some previous battle experience ar was quite agile, his long dark hair flying when l jumped up to kick you in the head. Edward ar Ashley were a couple of wise-crackers, but the seemed to be working hard.

Miranda selected one of her team to fig Rick in single combat. I had some trouble refrainir from holding my hands over my eyes and peekir through my fingers as Rick immediately w. pushed to the ground and pummeled by h opponent. Suddenly Andrew jumped in ar grabbed Miranda's kid, flinging him to the flo and pinning him by the neck.

"Enough!" Miranda yelled. The two kids c the ground quickly rolled over and jumped to the feet, breathing heavily. Miranda was obviously a k surprised to see anyone put up any sort of a fig against her team.

Next followed a lecture and demonstration self-defense skills. "You never want to let anyor get you on the ground," she admonished. "It's bett to run if you can, to stay out of your attacker grasp. And don't let them get you in a corner!"

By the end of the session, my kids were a much more adept at evading their opponents.

Miranda's kid was much more adept evading Andrew.

The competition would follow old-sty Olympic tae kwon do scoring rules. A blow to tl head would count two points, while a blow to tl body counted for one. Weapons and body arm were allowed, although it was not considered poli to kill your fellow student, unless by accident. So, eluding attackers was fine, but it wouldn't score any points. The competition would be quite different from training, but it was the best we could do.

At class later that week, I noticed that Rick had a few bruises that I hadn't noticed before.

I quietly inquired with Adamma about it after class. It appeared that evasion wasn't quite as easy in the dormitories. Miranda's star student Wes had engaged in a little extra training at Rick's expense.

I imagined that the presence of fellow students added to the humiliation.

"Don't worry, I've taken care of it," Adamma said. After the tournament I learned that a rather large black cat had crossed Wes's path on his way home after class.

The evening of the first competition, campus had a festive air. As everyone found seats in the stadium, trumpet fanfares blared forth and fireworks holos lit up the faces of the students. Another crowd of students watched the competition from the student union. The languages class had been pitching in all week to complete the dragon banner, and it was waving proudly at one end of the field, above simulated armies posturing with their assorted weapons.

Although our team fought valiantly, we lost that night, as well as every other competition the first year. I praised the team's perseverance and thanked them for the dragon banner. We had an identity now.

Gradually Dragon Team's resolve seemed to stiffen, and by the next fall, we were ready.

Pitched Battle

The dragon banner again sprang to life as tl team entered the arena. There was scattered poli applause and a few hoots from the student crowd.

The referee called for the team captains meet at the center of the battlefield. Dragon Tea had chosen Rick as captain in view of his illustriot family history, and I suspected the girls al; thought he had the most impressive armor. Ri donned his helmet and pulled down the faceguar A pair of deadly looking oryx horns jutted from tl temples. I had suggested to Rick that it might l cool to honor this long-dead Earth gazelle as part his battle regalia. Wes Mandela stepped forward f the other team, a feathered ostrich plume bobbir on top of his helmet.

A fanfare summoned the rest of the tean and their virtual armies. In addition to the actioı of the actual team members, scoring depended part on how the armies performed and we deployed. Dragon Team was well versed in virtu reality and holographic graphics, and we hɛ worked hard to increase the efficiency of tl programs in rendering realistic scenes. Ashley w especially proficient with this area, and was able use her cerebral cortex almost exclusively witho needing an assist from her more primitive pariet cortex.

Our strategy was to have Ashley devote mo of her energies to creating diversions and movir the army, while Rick and Andrew engage members of the opposite team in single combɛ Lightning flashed, followed by a clap of thund and a cold, soaking rain. Rick raised his saber ar feinted, but his hands were losing feeling, and tl weapon was becoming too slippery to handle. W

31

charged, and the sword flew from Rick's grasp. A gasp could be heard from the audience, and the announcer said, "Dragon Team loses a point to the Super Powers team!"

Ashley focused a beam of light onto Rick's sword and created a force field around it. He dived through the rain to pick it up and grinned with satisfaction when he could now grip it readily. *Nice work*, I thought, noting that the force field was designed to allow only Rick to reach through to pick up the sword. He waded forward, slashing in all directions.

Random slashing turned out to be a poor move, however. Wes was a skilled swordsman who had obviously spent a lot of time learning to parry, and he began to score points against Rick as he riposted each stroke.

"Switch to a stunner," I muttered, and then reconsidered. The rain would conduct the current in an unpredictable way.

Ashley added some capricious gusts to the weather mix, one of which pulled Wes off his feet. Rick stepped over him to administer a blow, but Wes applied a sweep kick to bring Rick down to his level...another groan from the spectators.

Wes elevated Rick to a vertical position and began generating a spinning lasso force field to immobilize him. It was beginning to look like the end for Rick. Wes began to strike Rick with a sharp switch, and the point count began to increase steadily as Rick winced with each blow.

Andrew stepped forward and said, "Release him, or I will give you the worst thrashing of your life!" Wes laughed and continued with the beating.

Pitched Battle

With Rick incapacitated by the glowing fiel it was fair for Andrew to engage Wes in sing combat. Andrew shouted to Ashley, "Get Rick o of there!" and executed a flying kick at Wes's head.

"Two points for Dragon Team," tl announcer intoned. Finally two points on the boar

The crowd roared and began to take a re interest. Wes drew his hand across his mouth ar stared at the blood on his hand. Even though wasn't real blood, it could be quite a shock to se especially if you were the victim...and it w probably Wes's first time.

Ashley furiously worked to dismantle tl force field, which was quantum encrypted. Luckil the students had access to the Erenarch Networ and usually they were smart enough to crack ev the most sophisticated safeguards in short orde She worked first to free Rick's hands. He beg bouncing up and down and jumped over to land blow on Wes's chest.

This must have disrupted Wes's control of tl force field, because it abruptly vanished.

Wes now had to choose which of the tw adversaries to face. Rick made the decision for hir shouting "Look ma, no hands!" and executing faithful imitation of Andrew's flying head kick.

"Now you're getting the hang of it," Andre grinned, and stepped aside to face another foe.

It took about another dozen skirmishes, b eventually Rick and Andrew were turning the tid The Dragon Team renewed its efforts with vengeance. When the final buzzer sounded, Drago Team was one point ahead.

Students poured onto the field and beg celebrating the upset victory, as the Dragon Tea waved its banner overhead. Spotting me, they yelled, "Hooray for Dr. C!" I can't describe how gratified I felt, although I tried to look modest. I also enjoyed having a nickname.

I glanced over at Miranda, who stood with Wes on the sideline wearing a stony expression. She knew that in real life, there was no buzzer to save one from an implacable enemy.

*****~~~~~*****

Chapter Four

Would It Kill You to Stop Doing That?

My second year as a teacher was going bett
than I had dreamed. After the tournament, w
celebrated our win in the student union with a fea
of delightful and unusual treats. I ordered up ɨ
many of the ingredients from the hilarious Celt
song, "Miss Fogarty's Christmas Cake" as the foc
synthesizer could reconstruct from its database:

> *There were plums and prunes and cherries,*
> *There were citrons and raisins and cinnamon, to*
> *There was nutmeg, cloves, and berries*
> *And a crust that was nailed on with glue.*
> *There were caraway seeds in abundance;*
> *Sure 'twould work up a fine stomach ache*
> *That could kill a man twice after eating a slice*
> *Of Miss Fogarty's Christmas cake*

The synthesizer didn't know what carawɛ
seeds were, and a few liberties were taken wi
"berries," including some Antipian flea berries, b
the class and I thought most of the ingredients we

very tasty. A sorry exception was citron, a foul and bitter candied rind of a lemon-like fruit. I made up a new recipe and entered that into the synthesizer, and they all ate happily, recalling Andrew's prowess and Rick's bravery. I tactfully brought up Ashley's and the rest of the team's contributions. Edward especially had shown great improvement over last season in handling fire weapons.

I always dipped liberally into the well of Celtic traditions for teaching, especially poetry and music. We sang a round of "Wavering Way," about a singer drunk on Ilean green brandy, which the students found uproarious.

As we settled in comfortably to eat, drink, and celebrate our victory, Adamma came over and asked me a question.

"Would it be all right to invite a friend, Dr. C?"

I said that would be fine, and she waved toward a dark corner across the room.

Much to my surprise, Adamma's huge black feline AI sprang into the light, flicking its tail and sniffing the air. A few of the girls from other classes shrieked and ran in the opposite direction.

Adamma stepped forward and said, "Don't worry, everyone. Serrahji is my friend. Here, would you like to pet him?"

A few of the students cautiously held out their hands and gingerly patted the big cat on the head. Serrahji growled and they jumped back.

Adamma laughed and said, "That's naughty, Serrahji. Now apologize."

Serrahji settled down at Adamma's feet.

The room slowly returned to normal as the students' curiosity about Serrahji got the better of

them and they started asking Adamma questior
How did she feed him? Serrahji was programme
to operate much like a biological cat, and neede
massive amounts of meat on a daily basis. Adamn
noted that she had a large balance in h
commissary account and could synthesize plenty
lean sirloin for her friend.

"He's a bit of a chore, though," she said. "Bao
home I had servants who did all the feeding ar
cleanup."

I asked how she had been permitted to brir
a wild animal to Erenarch Academy.

"Oh, he's not really wild," she said. "Actuall
he's a helper AI. It's customary for all of the roy
family to have guard animals. I've had Serral
since I was two."

Up until now, the other kids had considere
Adamma to be kind of a pest, chattering continual
and displaying entirely too much energy. She w;
often greeted with "Duh" when she asked one of h
fellow students what seemed like an obviou
question. She hummed a lot. The most comme
phrase she had heard in class was "Would it k
you to stop doing that?"

Adamma had been in line for the throne c
her home planet of Nioba, but her father had high
aspirations for her. He had pulled a lot of strings
get her into Erenarch Academy in spite of h
slightly   lower   intellectual   qualificatior
Apparently being royal was not an automatic ticke
but it was obvious to me that Adamma had what
took to be a leader. She had an unerring way
zeroing in on the questions that ordinary peop
would ask, annoying as that could be.

Now that they knew she would be bringing an awesome killing machine to class every day, the other students wanted to hear more about Adamma's home and customs. They edged closer to hear. Adamma began describing the luxuries and privileges she had enjoyed as a princess, impressing her new friends with tales of fancy clothes and easy wealth.

But she did not tell the whole story. When she had arrived at Erenarch last year at the age of only six, Donal assigned her to my class and called me in.

"Rowan, I want to share your new girl Adamma's circumstances with you. It is a rather bloody and morose tale, I'm afraid."

***

Adamma's father had not survived to see her admission to the academy. He had been the subject of more than one assassination plot, and a jealous family, most of whom desired the crown, surrounded him. King Mwinyimkuu ruled with an iron hand and punished his enemies swiftly and without mercy. More than one of his courtiers had vanished, as well as one of his more troublesome wives.

It was an obviously dangerous environment for an innocent young girl, in spite of the ubiquitous guards. Her uncle Gahiji had planted the idea in Mwinyimkuu's mind of sending Adamma away. Her father was suspicious of his younger twin, but he loved Adamma and started the wheels turning toward sending her to a remote, exclusive school off-planet.

The royal castle was a triple-towered pink sandstone edifice with walls several feet thick to block out the hot desert climate of Nioba ar withstand its intense windstorms. In spite of i rustic pueblo exterior, the castle was equipped wi the latest in physical comforts, such as son showers and holo furnishings. It also housed formidable communications and defense cent deep underground. Plush Capilene tapestri insulated the hallways and walls, many depictir famous historical victories.

Little Adamma spent most of her time in tl residential quarters, along with her mother and raft of female attendants. Once she learned to wal the attendants were kept busy chasing the toddl around as she explored the castle.

One day she slipped on a grey cape and too a leftward course down a long hallway. She hope she wasn't going to get lost, because her fath would get very angry with her. But her mission wi to find him before she was discovered.

She found her father in a large office in tl communications center. He was talking wi someone else, a holo person. (She adored holc You could stick your hand through them.)

"Daddy, can I come in?"

Looking a bit embarrassed, Mwinyimku excused himself from the hololink to Erenarch ar reached out to Adamma. There was no reason to l her know that he had been working on a way to g her out of harm's way. She crawled into his lap ar put her arms around his neck.

"What is it, my little one?" he said with slight smile. It was hard to keep a regal bearir with her around. Seeing her temporarily relieve the heavy burden of ruling, as well as the guilt l felt about confining her mother, Serena, to the residential sector.

Adamma's mother had ordered one of her courtiers to murder a politician who had the temerity to question one of Mwinyimkuu's decisions. When the secret came out, Mwinyimkuu had the power to pardon Serena, but instead he decided to incarcerate her under "house arrest."

The courtier, Ramatulal, disappeared.

Serena was infuriated by this treatment. She was of royal blood, and she felt she had a right to do what she pleased.

Mwinyimkuu told her, "Serena, those days of the crown having absolute power are over.

You can't murder my adversaries. You have to pay the price. Stay in your quarters. Or, I can banish you forever. What will it be?"

Serena submitted to the restriction, but grew increasingly paranoid as she imagined that her husband was plotting to kill her. Another of his wives had disappeared mysteriously, after all.

At least she still had her daughter. She would raise Adamma to be queen and she would be avenged. Although Adamma was just a little girl, she would be schooled in the ways of power and rule.

One night a scream rang through the residence. A servant had been delivering fresh flowers to the rooms when she tripped over the body of a courtier, a pool of his blood soaking the exotic carpet. A crowd rushed in to see Serena crouched in the corner.

"He tried to take Adamma," Serena cried. "Give me my daughter," she yelled at the silent body.

Mwinyimkuu was called, and he ordered physician to sedate Serena.

"Adamma was with me," he told her. "No o1 is trying to take her away."

He knew this was a lie, but he didn't want alarm Serena any further than was necessar Serena began to wander at night, despite beir sedated. Mwinyimkuu began to fear for Adammɑ safety, and commissioned Adamma's guardian A the gigantic black panther Serrahji.

Adamma was a light sleeper and hard needed more than six hours each night. One nig she was awakened by a low grumble from Serrah A brilliant flash of lightning, followed immediate by a booming thunderclap, made her bolt uprig from her bed. She rose and went out to explore, h bare feet soundless. Was it a ghost? She to another step.

Another lightning flash revealed her mothe approaching her with a dagger in hand. Adamn heard her mumbling incoherently, moaning, "Th little girl meant so much to me. Now I'll never s her again. Give me my daughter!"

With a tremendous roar a black shaɟ crushed Serena to the ground, sharp teeth instant ending her life.

"Mommy?" Adamma stood there in shoc her eyes wide. She couldn't breathe.

A dozen soldiers burst into the hallwɑ waving stunners, having been alerted by the AI.

They scooped up Adamma and retreate with the crying child.

Serena was buried as befits a quee Hundreds of black-clad mourners lined the dese route to the royal cemetery.

Mwinyimkuu returned to the communications center, alternately feeling chilled by the day's events and sweating from the serval-lined black velvet cape. He tossed it aside and ordered an emergency holo link to Erenarch. Hopefully the child was too young to realize her guardian had killed her mother.

Four years later, Adamma was packed and headed for Erenarch Academy. With a heavy feeling, Mwinyimkuu entrusted her to her spaceport escort team. Hoverboards were dispatched to carry dozens of packages into the hold of the transport. Adamma took a last look at her home, gathered her skirts, and trundled her case up the gangway. Serrahji padded behind, keeping the distance of an easy leap.

Mwinyimkuu watched from the castle as the ship rocketed upward in preparation to make the jump. He raised his arm to wave goodbye and felt a sharp sting in his back. Serena's courtier Ramatulal, long thought dead, screamed, "This is for my lady!" Strong hands pulled him away from the king, but not in time.

Adamma's uncle Gahiji contacted Erenarch about the second tragedy. It was decided not to tell her about her father's death. It would be several years before she learned of it.

Donal assigned Adamma her own dorm room, unlike most of the students, who got roommates. Thus none of her fellow students were privy to the times that she had nightmares, crying herself back to sleep with Serrahji as her pillow. She never feared him, sensing that he had saved her life, even if it meant taking her mother's.

***

I felt it was sad for the little girl to have
grow up so fast. By day, she was just a cheerf
little chatterbox who was proud to be at Erenarc
No one would have guessed that her dreams we
poisoned with a lifetime's worth of grim fortune.

I heard from Donal that things got better c
Nioba under uncle Gahiji's rule, but Adamma (ar
the rest of us at Erenarch) were never entirely su
whether he was implicated in her parents' deaths.
could have been a clever plan to usurp his twir
power, or perhaps he was merely in the right pla
at the right time.

*****~~~~~*****

Chapter Five

Super Furry Animals

With me well into my third year at Erenard Academy, we had studied a number of differe cultures and languages, and it was time to turn ou attention to other species.

A few planets in the system had chosen path different from AIs and made the consciou decision to augment native or animal species the considered beneficial, either genetically or via nar implants. On my home planet of Tarant, we ha bestowed this honor on "Man's Best Friend," th dog. We were largely agrarian, and dogs ha played a role in our Celtic ethos. We all knew th Welsh myth of Gwydion and Gilfaethwy, who we reincarnated as wolf dogs in retribution for the misdeeds. A good dose of being treated like a dc gave them a whole new perspective.

Mostly, though, dogs were great hunters ar loyal helpers. Centuries later, dogs still had plac of honor on the farm and hearth, even if only a pets.

My aunt had taken a liking to the sturc Welsh corgi, with its history as a little cattle dc with a big heart. She had four of them, all of whom had tracheal implants that let them pronounce words. The smartest, Tottles, had a working vocabulary of around two hundred words. Aunt Megan would give a whistle, and Tottles would load the sheep onto the glider for a daily spin around the fields of barley.

I wanted to introduce my class to an appreciation for the stewardship of other species as well as to instill the fact that this was one of the original ways we might someday cross the bridge to being able to communicate with alien species.

I gestured toward the silver trunk on my desk at the front of the room. A faint light glowed from inside, and a small fog of frozen mist sublimated into the air.

"Class, today I've brought in a half dozen frozen embryos that we are going to be growing. Each of you is going to come up with a plan to ensure that these embryos can grow up to do a certain task successfully."

"What are they, Dr. C?" Ashley asked.

"They are Canus Lupus Familiaris," I replied. Several students had never seen a dog. "For those of you unfamiliar with the species, they are dogs from my home planet, Tarant."

"Dogs! Cool!" Rick said. A low rumble issued from Serrahji, sitting next to Adamma.

Ever the practical one, Ashley asked, "What task are they supposed to perform?"

I grinned. "Cattle herding."

Rick said, "Where are we going to get cattle—and where would we keep them? It's fifty below zero outside."

"That will be part of the assignment. You m;
have to create some cattle-like creatures that like tl
cold, or you may want to design and build son
mechs that simulate big cows," I allowed. "Just l
sure to make them dumb enough that our litt
dogs can outsmart 'em."

"What kind of dogs are they?" Rick said. H
had obviously seen dogs before and knew the
were different breeds.

"Pembroke Welsh corgis," I said.

"Oh, great!" he exclaimed. "Those car
possibly herd cattle. They've got short little legs ar
are kind of fat and waddly looking."

"But they do have very big teeth," I replie
"It will be your job to train them to do the job, ar
you will be allowed genetic or nano modificatioi
as long as they conform to the proposed task. N
turning them into dragons or anything." I looke
pointedly over at Serrahji.

Some groans came from the class, but the
obviously were interested in turning their hand
something technical after months of linguistic ar
cultural studies.

"Just remember," I added. "You will l
graded on how well you bond with your corgi.

This is an exercise to see how you care fi
another species, how well you communicate with
and whether you can get it to work alongside yc
as a human."

I didn't go into detail about how dogs had
reputation for loving humans without reservatio
They would find that out themselves. I also didr
characterize the dogs as pets, since that mig
depend on whether the individual dogs could i
both roles, like my aunt's did.

"You'll proceed in teams of two," I said. "I'd like the proposed plans by this Friday, and the expected gestation will be one week following approval," I said.

***

Andrew's team turned in their proposal first, but all the class came through admirably with their plans. Andrew's included a genetic modification to add more hair to help the corgi withstand Erenarch's harsh climate. I pointed out that the corgi is naturally double-coated, but Erenarch was quite a bit colder than Tarant, so I approved the mods. The little creature wouldn't ever be a show dog, however, because "fluffies" were considered a fault by the judges.

Edward's proposal to lengthen his corgi's legs was rejected, because as I explained, the corgi was naturally bred to be low to the ground in order to dodge the cow's kicks. His partner Adamma's proposal to lower the pitch of the dog's bark and increase its volume was approved.

Rick wanted to add additional fast-twitch muscles to his pup's hind legs, to be done post-gestation. This too was approved.

Declan opted for lightweight heated body armor, in case his dog wasn't able to dodge blows from the massively larger cows.

Everyone agreed that Ashley should be the one to design the cow. She also offered to design an interface to a voice encoder that could be implanted in the pups to give them limited speech capability.

A week of furious work ensued, after which the pups were decanted.

"They're so cute!" Ashley exclaimed. She ha a gleam in her eye a little like a mad scientist as sh prepared the tiny vocoder chips for subcutaneou injection.

The six puppies were allowed to come class with the kids, and most slept quietly whi lessons took place. Their Celtic names were chose with care: the three males were Taliesin, Angus (al "Frankie"), and Bran. Bran, meaning raven, was looker, with a glossy black and tan coat and devilish grin. Taliesin was a ginger, a bit small fo his breed, with white fur around his tail in a hea shape that made him easy to spot at a distance. Th three females, all ginger and white, were Anwy (aka "Blondie"), Callie, and Pegeen (aka "Pearly").

For three months it was most housebreaking and frequent trips outdoors into th howling winter wind. By six months, most ha reached mature size. The males had also reache puberty, so the kids learned about birth contr methods used in animal husbandry.

Now the long wait ended as the puppi began their training.

Sometime during this period, Ashley notice that she couldn't keep up with her pup Franki who roared around with a lot of excess energy. Sh had nearly finished her cow, aptly named Cov which was a realistically sized robot that had limited AI. She had heard that cows had fou stomachs, which intrigued her. The resultir creature could eat anything organic and produced credible manure, which she donated to th Erenarch greenhouses. This gave her the idea making another big robotic creature, this time a all-white Earth horse. She could then ride comfort while Frankie caromed off hilltops and lifted his leg to spray fountains of pee that froze in the air.

This was just another example of Ashley routinely going above and beyond her assignments. The first time we saw Ashley on the horse, which she named Charger, it felt a bit like seeing the Celtic goddess Rhiannon ride out of the mist. The horse came in handy the next time we had a tournament battle as well. She even equipped Charger with gold armor that coordinated with Declan's little corgi, Tally. (I've got to admit Ashley was a teacher's pet.)

Rick and Bran were the first to start training. Bran's extra muscle had brought him to maturity more quickly than the others, though he still cut a trim figure in his youth. Bran looked over his shoulder at Rick and waited expectantly. Rick whistled, and Bran launched himself like a grinning heat-seeking missile.

"I knew he'd be a natural," Rick said.

"I think you made him a natural," I observed.

***

The training had shown the dogs were fulfilling their goals admirably, and the final trials were coming up soon. Spring was coming to Erenarch, but the weather decided to deal one last winter blow.

Declan and Taleisin were putting Cow through its paces when the snowstorm worsened into a blizzard. Declan could no longer see the cow or Tally, and whistled for Tally to come in. Declan's transponder had stopped receiving Tally's signal. Had his monitor stopped transmitting?

Declan came rushing in to the dome ar
announced that Tally was lost. We all tried to cal
him and began organizing a search and rescu
After all, we had five more dogs. These anima
were the original trackers before things lil
positioning systems were even invented.

Adamma wrung her hands and looke
worried while the students donned ext
outerwear. Serrahji paced back and forth.

"Adamma, you and Serrahji will stay here
coordinate and send help if more is needed," I sai
Serrahji quietly took his ease.

The students tethered their dogs to their bel
and set out into the shrieking squall wearir
heatsuits. As they crunched through the snow, the
footprints were quickly obliterated. Snow crysta
stung their faces, and frost clung to their eyelashe
After an hour, they were about to give up hoj
when Declan yelled that he had detected a fai
signal. The signal disappeared, then reappeare
stronger this time. They quickly followed, un
Frankie sounded the alarm with his pumped u
vocodor. He had discovered a cave where Tally ha
driven Cow for protection. It was hard to coax Co
from the back of the cave, but Frankie and Tal
finally pushed her out to where Ashley and Decla
waited. They covered Cow with a blanket and le
her away. Shivering and tired, Tally bumped u
against his master. Declan wrapped his cap
around Tally and hugged him to his body.

"Let's go, little buddy," he whispered.

A bedraggled crew of students and do;
stumbled into the student union, demandir
flagons of hot chocolate. The pups collapsed into a

untidy heap and immediately commenced to snore. That night the no-pets policy was not enforced.

The trials were moved indoors to the battle arena, and most of the school attended to see the brave little dogs that had survived the storm as they showed their stuff. I remember beaming and declaring, "Those guys are incredible!" as they barreled from side to side, biting at the heels of Ashley's cow. When Declan whistled, Tally let out his "I got it" bark and charged out to do cow battle.

When the unit came to an end, the class was awarded a First for their project. Little Declan turned to me with pleading eyes and asked, "Can we keep the little buggers permanently, sir?"

Sadly, the answer was no. But we shipped the dogs home to Aunt Megan on Tarant. Cold sleep for a bunch of pets was expensive, but she was a rich farmer. She became the new leader of the pack of the most gifted corgis in Dragon Stead.

*****~~~~~*****

Chapter Six

The Norns: Better Living Through Diversity

After all the excitement of getting lost in tl frozen wasteland of Erenarch and surviving wi the help of our canine friends, we enjoyed a year relative peace and quiet, and I finally was able return our future interplanetary leaders to ou scholarly studies.

Despite Erenarch's out-of-the-way location c the edge of the Sigma Draconis solar system, it w; the place where news of events occurring in the fa flung corners of the neighborhood poured in f(analysis. Erenarch Academy lessons tended to foct on the remote exploits of the Erenarch Networ while giving us what turned out to be a false sen; of security. Thus we were extremely fortunate have Donal Gray in our classroom the day tl Norns were considering whether to wipe out tl human species.

We were in the midst of our Governance un and my students were learning the whys and hov of Erenarch's existence. I wondered about how this chunk of ice was chosen as the capital planet of Dragon Stead in the first place. Erenarch was home to a consortium of like-minded planets that wanted to cooperate in providing security and resources for this small bit of the universe. Yet the individual planets each had their own governments, cultures, and ideas about how to live. A lot of thought had gone into the Articles of Organization of Erenarch, which had made it pretty successful as a charter for inter-government cooperation.

"What if we were going to design something like a town, a planet, or even a star system headquarters?" I posited. "Think of the motives that went into forming Erenarch to lead the Dragon Stead system."

"Do I get to be king?" Edward quipped.

"If your design is a monarchy, you'll have to specify how that will happen; who will be elevated, and how succession will be carried out," I replied with a straight face.

Erenarch was not a central government, but rather more of an alliance. It administered the Erenarch Network, the military/industrial communication arm of Dragon Stead. In a way, having an Erenarch Network made it easier for planetary societies to co-exist, since it could be called upon to step in to resolve emergencies. Although it hadn't been tremendously effective at preventing wars and lawlessness, at least it provided a relief valve for refugees and a military coalition with a fusion-powered fleet armed to the teeth with persuasive nuclear weapons. The Erenarch Network also housed a super powerful AI nicknamed "the Norns." The Norns kept track of

even minute details of every inhabited planet acro
Dragon Stead.

But on an everyday basis, most people didn
think about Erenarch. The things that affected the
most tended to be local. People wanted to kno
who their neighbors would be. Parents wanted
know how they were going to educate their kid
Farmers wanted to know how they were going
get their crops to market. City workers wanted
know how they would get to work. People wante
to know how to dispose of their trash—bas
survival issues.

"What are the pros and cons of usir
Erenarch as a base for humanity?" I asked. Ashle
noted that although Erenarch was a frozen plan
with little atmosphere, it was more Earth-like tha
not. The gravity and seismic and solar stability we
good, and there was a plentiful supply of froze
water and minerals.

"What about a planet with no water? Wou
that work?"

All agreed that it would be possible, b
exceedingly tough. I decided to invite a speak
who had experienced such conditions...my goc
friend, Donal Gray. His home planet had virtual
no water.

The next day Donal looked out over the clas
"My home town on Sharra imported all its water, s
we weren't farmers, that's for sure," he said. "But
good deal of the computing advances we use tod
came from the Sharran planetary region.

"We knew we needed to develop ne
assistive technologies that used no water. We I
upon the idea that, unlike humans, computers dor

use water to circulate stuff to their 'brains'—just electricity and quantum physics."

Robots and nanobots used designs provided by their fellow computers to construct more of themselves, and automation enabled a degree of terraforming that would accommodate both humans and machines. A number of new fluids and lubricants were invented that kept the machine species humming along. AIs were designed to recognize that humans were simply another intelligent species like themselves that required more specialized environmental conditions.

"We learned to take care of one another," Donal said. "AIs were subject to being knocked out by electromagnetic pulses, and we took care to shield them well. Likewise, we humans could withstand very little radiation, and the AIs finally worked out a way to shield both themselves and us from hard radiation, like gamma rays.

"We believe life originally crawled out of the sea on another planet, but when humans crawled into space, a lot of us died. Sharrans hoped that their society could consist of a range of species that could complement each other. It would be Earth-like in that respect, but quite different in the particulars."

"You mean non-biological, don't you?" Erik asked.

"In our case, it meant both biological and non-biological life," Donal agreed.

Questions poured from the class. Did a lot of humans die when machines didn't understand how delicate they were?

Donal replied, "One of the lessons the AIs learned from their biological neighbors was the advantage of diversity. They learned, for exampl that viruses were both a disease-causing organis and, more importantly, killers of most of tl bacteria on the planet. They began to emula constructs like viruses, and to engineer bacteria-lil organisms that were more beneficialto humans."

"So, is human life considered more importa than machine life? Who rules, man or machine Ashley asked.

"Admittedly, we do have some hierarch and humans are considered the 'creators' of Sharr⍺ life by the AIs. They know that we are not, course, but it is easier to deal with humans whe they do not feel threatened.

"Man rules the planet at a gross level, but tl AIs actually run things," Donal noted. "It's a matt of semantics."

Declan asked, "Did some of the robo resemble humans or other animals?"

"Yes, of course," Donal replied. "You all rec⍺ Ashley's horse design, don't you?" The cla laughed. A blood-chilling growl cut that short.

"And we're not forgetting you, Serrahj Donal said. "It's pretty common for Sharran kids design AI companions. When Dr. C. arrived, l looked a little homesick, so I created a little hobbi like creature to keep him company. He had a terrif sense of ironic humor."

"Yes, he was quite helpful during the drag⍺ banner competitions," I said. The class laughe again. The little robot had served draughts of wat to the combating students and shot off firewor volleys when our team scored.

"How long do the machines live?" Edwai asked.

"They do have limited lifetimes," Donal said. "But they have the ability to reproduce themselves, so they can clone themselves or otherwise bring more useful species to life. We ask them to limit themselves to Sharra and to not expand outward into the surrounding Dragon Stead.

So far they have honored that request."

Suddenly the air at the front of the classroom podium appeared to shimmer, indicating that an incoming holo or off-planet communication was imminent.

"Dr. Gray?" It was a holo of Donal's little robot. I stepped forward.

"What is it, Pippin?" I had named the AI after a character in an old pre-space travel myth.

It was fun to see him again.

"Greetings, doctors. I feel it is my duty to inform you that the Norns are preparing to take control of Erenarch. It is their view that humans are not necessary for the peaceful continuation of progress in the planetary system. In fact, humans' destructive tendencies continue to impede peace at every juncture."

The smiles on the students' faces faded and were replaced by looks of confusion.

Donal Gray was nominally the headmaster of Erenarch Academy, but he was also the chief system engineer of the Network and the designer of the Norns.

"Have the Norns been listening to my presentation?" he asked.

More shimmering occurred, then a trio of gray-haired women appeared beside Pippin...the Norns.

"Of course, Dr. Gray. We listen to ɛ communications."

Donal asked, "Would you do me the courteɛ of letting me complete my presentation befo terminating us?" he asked.

My former curiosity was replaced by feeling of terror as we awaited a response.

"Please continue, Dr. Gray."

"You had a question, Dr. C.?" he said, turnir to me.

"Ahem...ah, yes. Do the machines on Shar love or have religion?"

"Well, a machine can definitely have self ar other preservation programming," Donal said. "Bɪ they are also programmed to be extremely logicɛ Unless they are specialized, they do not tend write poetry or invent new religions, and a content to be partners with humans."

"But it sounds like they could have takɛ over if they wanted to," I observed, casting one eɪ toward the Norns. "They sound very powerfɪ Does that make Sharra powerful enough to ru Dragon Stead? What do Sharrans get by belongir to Erenarch?"

"Sharrans are like people everywhere," Don said. "Like you pointed out earlier, Dr. C., thɛ rarely think beyond their planet, unless there is big election coming up or a crisis to be dealt wit That goes for both the person-people and the ʌ people."

Donal bowed slightly and addressed tl Norns.

"Ladies, as you are undoubtedly aware, tl machine intelligence on Sharra is far superior that of Erenarch, but it has not chosen to revolt ɪ remove the biological entities there. In fact, the computational entities have helped humans transcend their biological limitations. Thus, there is little fear of humans on Sharra."

Donal explained that with the AIs handling the basic creature comforts on Sharra, it was fascinating to see that the daily interaction with their human neighbors became the main concern of AIs on Sharra. Biological cleansing would not be permitted, he added.

"We all share in the blessings of intelligence, some more than others, of course," Donal added.

We all laughed nervously.

"Indeed, you are referring to the different Ways of Knowing," the Norns replied.

The Norns still didn't seem totally convinced that as superior intellects they should continue working with humans. Sharra might be peaceful, but other planets constantly caused problems. Donal argued persuasively that it would be in the mutual interests of the Norns to raise the various strains of humanity's awareness to a higher level, and that they could play a key role. After conferring with each other, they decided to defer to their creator's analysis.

"We are grateful for your presentation, Dr. Gray. We better understand the importance of diversity in fostering civilization. Would it be possible to further integrate with the Sharran intellect, Dr. Gray? This would greatly enhance our confidence for the future."

All eyes turned toward the little Sharran-designed robot as it hobbled forward with the verdict.

"I'm hearing that's a roger from Sharra," I said.

We all breathed a collective sigh of relief.

*****~~~~~*****

Chapter Seven

The Loss of Anberra

The close call with human annihilation k
AIs led to a shakeup of the Erenarch Network. Soc
after the Norn AIs decided to renew their allian
with humans, the Network received a raft of ne
job applications. One was from Hilly Gerhart, o
math teacher.

Hilly had oftentimes recounted, over a bee
his failure at inculcating our students with what I
considered even the most basic computer scien
lessons. "They don't even understand numeric
methods of integration," he would moan. "There a
a few exceptions, like Ashley," he would conso
himself.

Thus, when it was announced that tl
Network would undergo major upgrades, it was r
surprise that Hilly requested a transfer.

Donal had been one of Hilly's few friends. F
tactfully said, "We'll miss you a lot, Hilly, but
think you have the right temperament, not
mention Sharran background, to make a gre
contribution to the Network."

I agreed with Donal. Hilly was not really good with people and struggled as a teacher.

He'd be much happier making friends with the Norns. They would understand him.

In some respects, the Norns had been right. We humans often did some stupid things.

When I gratefully was able to return our future galactic leaders to their scholarly studies, I immediately thought of blue Anberra and how our actions led to its loss.

I decided to sidle up to the topic by casting the Anberran environmental disaster as a dusty old historical event.

"Today's topic is lost languages," I said. Over time, many languages evolved to meet the needs of their civilizations, while others died out. A few had been lost due to the sudden demise of the whole civilization. I assigned Rick to do a report on the loss of the planet of Anberra about two hundred years earlier. The planet still existed, but no one lived there anymore, and its climate was inhospitable. I asked Rick to research how many languages there had been on Anberra and how many had survived, if any.

A few days later, Rick gave his presentation. We sat back and listened with increasing dismay as he recounted what went wrong on Anberra.

Oceans largely covered Anberra, and surveyors found cold polar regions, temperate regions with snow, and warm tropical regions. It was the first planet settled in Dragon Stead and the most Earth-like. Unfortunately, it had high volcanic activity, which caused bouts of climatic cooling, alternating with high releases of greenhouse gases that began warming the planet. Melting of ice

sheets led to shortages of fresh water. Ironically,
also led to massive flooding of the coastal area
Ocean currents began to reroute themselve
Previously semiarid regions turned into dust bowl
Gigantic dust storms flattened everything in the
paths. Salts built up on the soil, severely impactir
agriculture. Gradually, it became necessary
synthesize all food, an energy-intensive ar
expensive proposition. Large die-offs of speci
began as habitats were lost.

At first, the majority of people ignored tl
climate changes and consequences predicted l
computer simulations. Although disasters we
increasing, they did not directly affect most peopl
At any rate, people believed that climate chang
could be mitigated with technology and th
scientists were predicting doom unnecessaril
Simulation after simulation continued to sho
various regions were changing, mostly for tl
worse. Oceans were increasingly acidic. It was
little like putting a lobster in warm water ar
gradually turning up the heat.

As Rick explained, "It's easy to confu:
climate with weather, too. The climate chang
were gradual and over a long term, but they we
also responsible for causing more extreme weath
events.

"There were a lot of big destructive weath
events along the coasts, like hurricanes ar
cyclones, but the predictions were not alwa
precise. So, it was hard to get people to leave the
homes or take shelter in advance. In fact, peop
would go outside to see if they could see a tornac
or hurricane coming. Not too bright, but thal
human nature," Rick said.

Some attempts were made to sequester gases below the ocean floor and to seed the oceans with iron oxide nanocrystals that would scavenge carbon from the atmosphere. It became increasingly costly to modify the climate enough to re-create conditions that used to support the population of a nearly a billion humans. The prospect of moving everyone underground seemed unavoidable, and people began fighting for living quarters below the surface.

Gradually the population became tired...tired of waiting for a day without crises, tired of waking up every morning to hear more bad news, tired of searching high and low for more solutions. People became ineffably sad, and some didn't want to wait to die. The suicide rates rose. Other planets in the quadrant could see the writing on the wall and began planning for an influx of immigrants.

The problem was, it was not feasible to transfer a billion people. Nearby planets were just getting established and had limited resources. Interplanetary relocation was arduous and expensive, requiring construction of thousands of nuclear pump drives and facilities for putting passengers into cold sleep. A number of Anberrans did accomplish their mass exodus successfully, though, thanks to the sacrifices made by many, plus the intervention of Erenarch Network.

One volunteer was a young Erenarch Academy graduate sent there to facilitate emigration. Rana Thorvaldson was shocked when he landed in the port city of New Sydney to find that a cult of death and deprivation had taken hold. Citizens who agreed to starve or otherwise stop

using scarce resources were being "rewarded" wi
the ability to upload their consciousness ar
memories to AIs. It seemed like a practical solutic
for continuing to live on a planet whose climate w.
too harsh for humans.

As he walked the corridors of tl
underground sanctuaries, Rana was bombarded l
broadcasts and holos urging him to give up h
dreary life and join the millions who ha
successfully uploaded to the data banks. He use
his Erenarch authorization to request a visit to
data bank. The director, Alasdair McQueen, resiste
giving Rana access.

"I don't know why Erenarch Network thinl
it can meddle in our affairs," he said resentfull
"We are an independent planet with autonomy."

Rana went over McQueen's head to the hea
of the government to obtain access. He pointed o
that Anberra was a member of the Network, ar
that gave him authority to assess the situation.

"I've been hearing so much about the:
citizens who are uploading to the data bank. I'd lil
to meet one."

Unfortunately, when Rana finally gaine
access there was no one to meet. McQuee
grudgingly revealed that the data from each citize
was being preserved, but there were no plans fi
reactivating anyone. Thus, none of these AI citizei
were living any kind of life. They were
permanent hibernation.

No physical DNA was being kept, and the
bodies were being disposed of. To Rana's horror, l
found that relatives were discouraged fro
establishing memorial parks or keeping oth

mementos and remains, because these took up valuable underground space and resources.

As people increasingly lost loved ones, the sense of despair grew. Anberra was gradually forgetting its history and people.

Rana contacted Erenarch to report his findings. The administration in turn contacted the relatively nearby planet of Farana to see if it would agree to take charge of Anberra's data banks.

The interplanet transfer had just been agreed to when McQueen caught wind of it.

McQueen declared, "We in New Sydney will not tolerate having the Erenarch Network steal our virtual population!"

He persuaded the city government to establish martial law, which forbade any of the remaining people in New Sydney to try to immigrate. The New Sydney council decreed further belt-tightening, instituting roundups of citizens "who were not contributing to society." New Sydney declared that these citizens were destined for upload, "until conditions for humanity on the planet improve."

Meanwhile, McQueen secretly ordered the destruction of the New Sydney data bank.

Rana went in under cover to one of the upload centers, where about one thousand people were waiting for the procedure. Looking around, he saw that a large proportion of the uploadees were families with young children. This couldn't be right. He activated his communicator and was about to report the violation to Erenarch when he felt his legs buckle under him as a stunner bolt struck from behind. Paralyzed, he could only watch as the others in the room also dropped to the ground.

White-coated personnel walked around, ostensib uploading data from each person, while uniform< soldiers loaded bodies onto antigrav stretchers.

"Rana Thorvaldson was only one of sever million people lost on Anberra," Rick said.

"But thanks to his courageous effort Erenarch was aware immediately of what w< going on in New Sydney. Everything he saw w< transmitted back to the Network, until it all we: black."

Troops from other cities were dispatched New Sydney for humanitarian aid, and Erenar< launched a battalion that arrived a few months lat to further quell McQueen's coup of the legal ci government.

Thorvaldon's sacrifice had been two hundre years ago. Since humanity had harnessed fusic power, we had been quite successful at creatir islands of plentiful energy and breathab atmosphere, and could usually synthesize what v needed to live, even in poor climates. Our capital Erenarch was like that—we lived in a bubble on planet that was normally too cold for humans live there comfortably. Currently, we could al: move much greater distances, and many of tl Anberrans did accomplish their mass exodt successfully.

But it was a tragedy when dozens of oth established species died, some of which could hav evolved to sentience themselves. Most of tl evidence of human civilization on Anberra w< gone since raging fires had consumed tl continents.

I asked, "What about the languages Anberra? Were they lost?"

Rick replied, "There were about fifty human languages there. Not as many as on old Earth, because Anberra was only settled about three hundred fifty years ago. As people moved away, they began speaking the languages of their new home planets. Fires destroyed most physical record repositories in the native Anberran languages.

"Luckily," he continued, "the arrangements to stream the data banks off Anberra to orbiting data stations worked well. However, the population pressure on nearby Farana was intense as refugees flooded in. It probably contributed to the nasty war that broke out."

I observed that most people couldn't read or understand the Anberran records without consulting a specialist in ancient and obscure languages. I myself only knew two Anberran dialects among the thousand or so total that I spoke.

Ashley asked, "And what about the virtual people in the data banks?"

"Most of the citizens were restored to human bodies through cloning," Rick reported. "Of course, they weren't their original bodies, but they were able to get bodies that were similar to what they remembered."

"Ha, I'd remember having a much better-looking body if it was left up to me," Ashley joked.

The class concluded that the lesson of Anberra was that the population was too shortsighted to preserve what it had before it became too late. Then the population was too large for Anberra to support, even with their best technology.

***

The Loss of Anberra

Under the right—or wrong—conditions, w
could all be lost like Anberra due to our inability
take proper care of the natural and technologic
creations we were blessed with. The shock was ho
quickly things could go downhill.

It has been nearly forty years since Rick ga\
that report on Anberra. Plantlike AIs have bee
seeded onto the surface and are reporting back
Erenarch about climate conditions. It is expected
take another one thousand years before tl
atmosphere regains an equilibrium similar to tl
original conditions before human settlement. It
hoped that one day it may be possible to r
introduce a small human population, protected by
support system that could cope with the plane\
volcanic temper. We may even find that son
native species survived. But in the meantime, w
grieve for the beauty of what was once blu
Anberra.

As the great poet said,

Where are the snows of yesteryear?

*****~~~~~*****

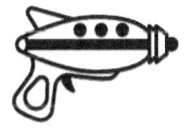

Chapter Eight

War Beckons

As a teacher at the Academy, I knew that m students might be going off planet, sometimes virtual diplomats and other times as physic combatants, and lessons such as the fall of Anber had impressed the duty of vigilance upon us all. M job was to facilitate my students' evolution leaders. Unstated, but also evident, was my role discouraging untoward attachments and in pushir them toward their duties as intellectual leaders Erenarch.

In this I was entirely unsuccessful.

***

My older boys in that first class were turnir seventeen when word came of another crisis on tl Faranan colony. Diplomatic missions had thus f failed, and Erenarch was putting tl supercomputer to work planning f "interventions" under a dizzying array of scenario

Ashley and Edward were requisitioned assist in the programming effort, although Ashle was far more capable than Edward. Edward w. probably chosen because his personality profile w.

somewhat bellicose. He would not add a great deal of negotiation skills to the tactical mix. He had always chafed at being at the Academy, because he felt more suited to military leadership and would have preferred to be an agent of the Network. As he had grown to his teen years, he had become a strapping young man with a commanding presence. He used every opportunity to apply for training at Network Command.

Ashley was best friends with Edward and loyally supported his aspirations, often helping him with programs that helped him win competitions in the school. Edward in turn felt that Ashley's devotion was his due, and he treated her as a close compatriot. I would often see them huddling together laughing as they put together a particularly vicious program to devastate opponents.

"Pretty cool, eh?" Ashley said, as holos of exploding planet parts rotated in the air in front of them. "Want some popcorn?"

Edward grabbed a handful and munched thoughtfully. "Yeah, but look at this popcorn.

Some of the kernels didn't pop. What if a planet is like that? What if we missed some terrain, or they launched lifeboats before the detonation?"

"No problem," Ashley said. "We'll just use fresher popcorn," she joked.

The source of the crisis was a planet called Farana. Farana had a largely human population, but had experimented heavily with crossbreeding with other indigenous species there. Most humans in the Dragon Stead were tolerant of genetic enhancements that would help survival on some of the planets that were not completely hospitable to human habitation. However, this was most minimal, and humans depended on technology provide comfortable habitations, as was done c Erenarch.

On Farana, an influx of immigrants fro Anberra a few hundred years earlier had pu strain on resources and encouraged further genet tinkering. Farana was extremely successful improving its inhabitants' strength, intelligenc and aggressiveness. This led to a new religic whose major tenet was Faranan superiority.

A religious aristocracy, rather than the mo prevalent secular bureaucracy, led the ma continent of Narasia. Narasia began to enterta imperialistic tendencies and raised a large arm eventually ruling all of Farana. Farana beg dispatching missionaries around the Dracan rir Recruits were promised genetic enhancements th would give them advantages, as well as land ar resources from planets that were absorbed into tl Faranan alliance. A raid on the relatively bucol planet Iles de Saintes came as a complete surpri and was the start of Farana's fledgling empire.

As dispatches reached Erenarch, Edwar followed these developments with keen interest.

He begged to be allowed to go under cover a Faranan recruit. Although already large ar formidable by human standards, he was qui willing to undergo genetic transformations th would allow him to embed himself into Farar culture, where he could better impede Farana intentions.

"Erenarch Command is the only thir standing between Faranan aggression ar freedom," he would say. He was eager to fight for Erenarch Network Command.

Ashley agreed with Edward's assessment, but worried about his desire to participate directly. She made it clear she did not want to see him go, possibly to be in harm's way. Ashley began to wait for him to finish his daily workouts so she could accompany him to the student union. She brought him little gifts and offered to do his history analyses. Many of the other students assumed they were a couple, except for Edward, who treated her like a little sister. He would accept her offers with a hug and dismiss her with a quick kiss, leaving her weak-kneed and blushing.

Ashley bragged about a package that had arrived at her door, containing an obsidian bracelet embedded with remote communicators. She had talked all semester about what she would do if she could ever afford one. The card said only, "From a secret admirer." Obviously, he must love her! Ashley's pleas for Edward to stay at Erenarch to help with the strategic management of the crisis became increasingly urgent.

Supporting Ashley, Andrew also questioned the wisdom of Edward's plan to join the Army undercover. Andrew and I came upon them having a heated argument about the conflict and what to do about it.

"I think Ashley's right," Andrew interrupted. "It would be better to leave this to a trained operative. Undercover work would require a cool head, which is the opposite of what you've got."

That was true. Although trained in weapons and defense, Edward had often gotten himself into

scrapes with Miranda's minions, from whic
Andrew had had to extricate him more than once.

Ashley angrily retorted, "You don't kno
what you're talking about. Butt out."

Andrew responded, "You sound like you'
blindly in love and that Edward can do no wron
You aren't at Erenarch to find a husband, yc
know."

Ashley shook her wrist bracelet to close h
computer session and pointed at Andrew, saying,
told you. Get out!" Sobered by this chastisemer
Andrew withdrew, and I scurried along behin
Andrew seemed to be reaching the conclusion th
it was a mistake for him to be in love with Ashley.

I talked with Donal and discussed Edwarc
proposal to go to Farana and join the religiou
movement there. Donal and I went looking f
Edward and found him in the gym, jugglir
multiple fire spheres.

"Edward, can we talk with you?"

Edward continued juggling.

"I understand that you wish to go to Farar
as a Network agent. Is that right?"

Edward stopped juggling briefly. "Yes."

"Can you tell us why you want to go the
rather than staying here and handling the cris
response?"

"I love Erenarch and all it stands for," Edwar
said, setting the spheres spinning again. "I want
be Erenarch's eyes and ears on the ground."

"But isn't that dangerous?" I interjected. "Wl
not leave it to the trained operatives? I'm sure the
would follow your orders."

"I don't want to just sit in a chair while peop
are dying. Surely, it would benefit Erenar

Command to have a battle-trained leader. Besides, I've waited all my life for this."

He was battle trained, but he wasn't battle experienced. I feared he was simply being naive. But his motives seemed pure.

Donal grew pensive but at last accepted Edward's plea.

Edward positively glowed as he made travel preparations. Ashley walked around with red-rimmed eyes and scowled at the other students who looked admiringly at Edward as he prepared to leave. Within a few weeks he was waiting to board the shuttle to the spaceport.

Ashley stood there stoically as Edward punched her in the arm and asked her to wish him luck. Then she threw her arms around him and turned to walk away. Embarrassed, Edward boarded the shuttle. I tried to console Ashley by telling her not to worry, and that they were too young to be in love.

I later regretted my role in discouraging Ashley's love for Edward. Erenarch prevailed, as expected. But a year after Edward's departure, we learned that he had been killed on Farana in a large battle, laser beams piercing both of his genetically enhanced hearts.

*****~~~~~*****

Chapter Nine

Down With War

I was still a young teacher when the Farana war began. Although that adventure wa eventually put down, there had been a series wars, some nastier than others, as quadrants Dragon Stead slipped back into barbarity.

Ashley was devastated when she heard th Edward had been killed. Andrew tried to comfo her but was given the cold shoulder whenever l approached. She gazed sadly at her bracelet, whic was the last memento she had of Edward.

Andrew also began to withdraw from tl class, spending more and more time in the gy training with Miranda Powers and her goons. didn't know if it was because he was trying impress Ashley, but if so, it wasn't working.

***

Miranda may have been shocked t Edward's death also, but she didn't appear total surprised. She doubled the defensive training of h kids, and put them through even harsh conditions, if that was possible. More than o1

79

student went around with temporary stitches and dislocated noses. The medical team could patch them up quickly, so it wasn't necessary to wear stitches, but her students were proud to have scars to show off. They could always be erased later.

The tournament this year was going to be fiercer than ever, with the Faranan conflict and Edward's death in the back of everyone's minds. I herded my charges over to the training field to take advantage of Miranda's recently expanded training hours.

Miranda spied Andrew, and she quickly surmised that something was troubling him.

"Problems, kid?" she said to him.

"No, ma'am. I'm good," he replied.

"Don't call me ma'am. I'm not your mother," Miranda said. Andrew had to agree that Miranda was nothing like his mother.

***

While it was pretty common for kids to have crushes on teachers, Miranda Powers had no trouble in that department. All the boys and not a few girls were drawn to her like pins to a magnet. She came to the Academy quite young, probably only a few years older than some of the senior students, and possessed a tough, rebellious exterior that she projected in her martial arts instruction. One day I learned how she became so versed in the art of war.

My annual retelling of the Ring myth had made quite an impression on my students, so I once attempted to score some points with her by mentioning that she looked like one of Wotan's warrior maidens from Norse mythology. With her long dark braids and Kevlar body armor, she did

80

have the appearance of a heroic Valkyrie. Instead
being flattered, she skewered me with a fierce glar

"I don't want to drag heroes off the battlefie
to Valhalla," she declared. "I want to make sure tl
heroes don't get themselves killed in the first place

"I may dress like a Viking," she added. "B
these braids would have gotten me killed.

Easy to grab while somebody runs yc
through with a broadsword."

Miranda was from Daris Prime, whe
violence was commonplace. I was something of
pacifist, so I worried about the message she w
sending to students. If I were being truthful wi
myself, though, the Academy valued h
curriculum more than the literary arts. Luckily fi
the likes of teachers like me, the inherent value
science and technology had also made a
impression on humanity.

One evening when Donal and I were havir
a drink at the student union, Miranda appeared
the door. Making complete fools of ourselves, v
waved wildly at her and finally caught her eye. V
asked her to join us, and she allowed as how sl
could sit for a bit.

I immediately began asking her abo
attitudes on Daris. Her deepening frown made
evident that she thought I was an idiot, and
squirmed in my seat. Donal shot me a sidelong gr
and stepped in to save the situation. He had hire
her, so he knew some of her history.

"I've really been impressed with the progre
you're making with the military strategy unit," I
told her. "What approach have you been taking
He knew the answer perfectly well, but he w
asking this for my benefit.

"It's all an issue of establishing healthy boundaries," she said. "Everybody needs some personal boundaries, and that's where the self-defense and martial arts come in. But countries and planets need to be able to live safely too."

"But isn't having a war over a line on a map kind of pointless?" I asked.

"Not if it's the only way to repel a bully," Miranda replied. "I believe firmly in using diplomatic methods where possible. However, that's a different branch of Erenarch Network, and they keep us in the loop on a Need-to-Know basis. If things get beyond diplomacy, we are there to minimize the bloodshed where possible."

"Why hasn't that helped on Daris?" I stubbornly and foolishly persisted.

"I think it is helping, but it takes time to change a whole culture. It's like a contagion. Left to its own devices, Daris would eat Tarant and your foppish medievalists for breakfast. You should be grateful the Network has a tight leash on Daris. It's another Faranan conflict waiting in the wings."

The "healthy boundaries" remark rang a bell with me. Miranda had shocked and outraged a lot of her fellow teachers when she went to extremes to provide her students with realistic battle scenes, complete with dead, stinking bodies, flies and maggots, and plenty of gore. A lot of the bodies wore garb from peaceful planets like Tarant in Iles de Saintes.

"Look into the crystal ball, people," she had said. "This is what your planet is going to look like if you don't establish healthy boundaries." I never said she was politically correct. She was simply reminding us civilized types of the dangers uncivil behavior.

I later realized Miranda was more tha patient with dolts like me. She had nearly n survived her childhood on Daris, living hand-t mouth and suffering the indignity of being helple against the abuse of family and enemies alike. Sl was only ten years old the day she discovered stun weapon on a corpse lying in the street. Lucki it was pointing in the right direction when sl curiously pressed her finger against the red circle.

A blue spark jumped out from the stunne and a chunk of concrete exploded from the concre wall next to her. It had been set to deliver a dead blow to anything in close proximity.

The hole looked familiar, just anoth pockmark in all the buildings in the neighborhoo Miranda saw the small green button and pushe that. Nothing happened...apparently that was tl safety.

She clipped the stunner onto her belt ar pulled her shirt out to hide it. It was getting late, she knew she needed to get off the street.

She had waited a little too long. A group teenage boys was coming around the corne laughing loudly and bragging about the old coup they had just mugged. Here, to their delight, w fresh meat.

"Hey, little girl, where you headed?" tl leader said. "What's that under your shirt?" He p his arm around her neck.

Miranda didn't reply and tried to pull away.
"Let's see what you got," the leader said.
Miranda twisted and ducked out of his gras The stunner found its way to her hands. Sl

pressed the red button without thinking. The boy fell to the ground, twitching.

"Get away from me!" she screamed. The other boys held out their hands and backed away. As she ran down the street, she realized she hadn't killed him. The red button had a low setting.

That night, when she went to bed without any supper yet again, she hugged the stunner tightly against the cold night and stared sleeplessly into the dark. Instead of dismally pondering the possibility of food tomorrow, as she usually did, she felt herself float dreamlike into a sunlit vision in which a crowd of ragged onlookers parted for a young woman warrior wearing a stunner on her belt. The woman climbed aboard a space transport and left Daris far behind.

***

For years after the Banner competition, Miranda's battle training sessions had attracted a crowd of students who filled the gym bleachers. The north end of the gym was kept empty, as a safety area to contain the occasional explosion and billowing smoke. Because the Dragon Banner Team did so well at the competition, I think Miranda tolerated my kids much more than previously.

She revealed a small chink in her armor by deigning to help Andrew, and she tended to treat him with the same disrespect as her best students.

Andrew kept his hurt at being spurned by Ashley close to his vest, but Miranda helpfully devised a lot of ways that he could let off steam. She continually drilled them, "Don't get mad. Just get even."

One evening Donal, Miranda, and I were having a drink at the student center. Miranda was saying how she liked Andrew's fighting style. I sa: I was worried that he had showed little reaction Edward's death. All the other students were actin quite upset.

"It's not that he doesn't have feelings, but l is supremely sensible," she said. "He isn't afraid retreat when he knows he's outgunned. That w keep him alive."

Years later, she was proven right, of cours Andrew enlisted in the Faranan conflict and, durir the next series of clashes, he distinguished himse as the hero of more than one battle, and he lived tell about it...not that he did. It was usual Classified. It was unfortunate that his friendsh with Ashley seemed permanently broken.

I was not so sure about Miranda's stateme: about Andrew's training, and was mulling it ov along with the excellent spiced wine, when I heai a big commotion near the entrance. It looked lil some yelling and shoving was going on. We stoc up to get a better look and to see if we needed break something up.

We did. Ashley and a number of oth students were taking over the student center.

"Stop the war!" Ashley shouted. "Erenar keeps the peace. Do your job!"

Miranda raised an eyebrow, a big reaction fi her.

"Quit sitting around on your hands!" Ashle urged. "Join us to put an end to this insanity. Oi people are dying out there, and Erenarch is doir nothing to stop it!" Her friends were whoopir assent and encouraging other kids to join them.

"We're not leaving until the administration agrees to our demands," Ashley added, sitting down and crossing her arms.

"Whoa, what about that?" I said, turning to Donal.

Donal was nowhere in sight. I guessed that was because he was the administration.

I finished off my mug and beat a hasty retreat as well.

The next morning, no one was in class. I was fairly certain all my fellow professors were in the same boat, as there was a huge crowd spilling out the doorway of the student center common room. I could hear the chants of "No More War" becoming louder as I approached.

The chants changed to "Ashley! Ashley!" as she came out onto the quadrangle. They quieted somewhat when she began to speak.

"I know we're young, and they probably don't want to listen to us, but we are the ones who are on the line," she said. "I just lost one of the best friends I've ever had, and it's a huge loss to Erenarch. We are the future leaders of the Network, and it's time for us to step forward."

Ashley and the other students continued to hold the student center hostage for the next week, with little sign of letting up the pressure on the Academy administration.

Finally Donal stepped up and told everyone it was time to clear out.

"Listen, I know how you feel. We've all suffered a horrible loss with Edward. But it's our duty to continue learning new and better ways to keep the peace. It's a big solar system out there, and we can't always know every detail. I think the

Network is doing a pretty good job, and you your people are key to programming the Norns to let u know about problems. You're also our best ar brightest for negotiating truces and eventu treaties.

"Don't let this incident cause you to lo: hope. Although it may not seem like it, I thir things are getting better. We are having few disastrous wars. Humans everywhere are livir more secure lives, thanks to you. Sometimes l being part of the Erenarch Network, we can forg this, because we may not see it firsthand.

"So, I've invited some people from Farana speak to you today, and I hope you will give the some of your time," Donal said.

The air in front of the crowd shimmered, ar a group of holo people materialized.

Somebody had sprung for a lot of credits establish this hyperlink from billions of miles awa\

"Hello, Ashley. I am Morgana Renitier president of Farana. It's an honor to speak to yo We want to thank you and Erenarch for all yc have done to bring peace back to Farana. I reali: that since I am also head of the church of Farar that I played a role in letting this conflict get out of hand, so if you don't want to listen to me will understand. I have brought many of our oth citizens so you can hear about their experienc firsthand. I am so sorry for your loss."

Another person stepped forward.

"Hi, Ashley and Erenarch. Greetings fro Tarant, Iles de Saintes. I am Brandon L'Estrang and I led the rebellion after Farana invaded. We a finally getting back to normal, and this is all thanl to your efforts. I did not know the boy who went

Farana on our behalf, but we will remember him with a monument in our principal town. We are so grateful to be able to go back to our relatively carefree farming way of life."

He turned to the holo of Morgana.

"And thank you, Madame Renitiere, for tolerating our different lifestyle."

She smiled and lowered her head.

Other holo people who had lost loved ones came forward and reached out to Ashley. Tears were streaming down her face as she held out her palm to touch their transparent hands. Other students solemnly moved in a line to reach out to the virtual visitors from other worlds.

The students had lost a treasured classmate, and they were being asked to put their grief behind them. Amid much sniffling and some grumbling, Ashley and her pals eventually dispersed and returned to class.

Erenarch continued to cast itself as a disinterested observer of planetary affairs, avoiding taking sides but applying force and negotiation when it saw fit. While Network Command military had taken the brunt of casualties in the defense of the invaded territories, I had also seen more of my students die in her service. I only came to realize this gradually, since Erenarch Academy trained strategians rather than warriors, but many a diplomat had risked death over the years.

Andrew told me later that when he was in the field with bloodshed and brutality occurring all around him, he would always muse on his Academy days.

"It seemed strange that life went on as usual back at Erenarch while we were fighting just to stay alive out there. It's like another world." Which was.

Although more wars had occurred since tł Faranan conflict, it became less likely that innoce civilians would die in wars, with machines, Al and computers doing much of the battling, but tł stakes were high, and losing could mean seriou disruptions and even having to move off-plan while basic infrastructure was restored.

*****~~~~~*****

Chapter Ten

War's End and New Beginnings

One of the most astonishing moments
recent human history was the discovery of a bein
who had been in stasis for a million years. A tea
of miners extracting some lithium salt on a moon
Daris broke through the crust to a subterranea
lake of frozen water. There they encountered a
object that was even colder than the ambient on
hundred degrees Kelvin; dangerously close
absolute zero, in fact. The box seemed to displ
quantum effects such as superconductivity an
superfluidity, effects that we normally on
encountered in the manufacture of AIs. The mine
had a hard time getting a grip on the container, as
seemed to resist attempts to attach to it. It repelle
machines that drove close to it, adjusting i
magnetic field from momentto moment.

Eventually Erenarch decided to build
structure around the artifact rather than trying
remove it, since it was not clear what, if anythin
was inside.

The activity around the site must have alerted the occupant, however, as it began to generate spin waves that caused it to disappear. There was bedlam for a while as panicking scientists tried to discover what had happened. The humans retreated several thousand kilometers, leaving AIs in charge of probing the site's environment. Analysis seemed to reveal that the artifact was still present, although perhaps in a slightly different time or dimension.

My Celtic imagination ran away with me, as I pictured a big river monster waiting to be released from its prison. Was it Morgawr from the future? Would our kids live to tell about it? Would our kids exist at all? That was part of what was frightening about the discovery, knowing that the future could be meddling with us. Time travel for us up to that point had been limited to looking at the very immediate past, like a few split nanoseconds ago.

The AIs on-site were the first to communicate with Old Abraham, as he became known, broadcasting messages of peace on a variety of wavelengths.

The being remained silent for a disconcerting amount of time, but then we all heard it speak, from within our own heads, it seemed.

"I am pleased to meet you all, and I am happy to see that you have treated your creations well."

I assumed he meant the AIs on Sharra. Maybe the AIs assumed he meant their engineering creations. We all probably assumed what we wanted most to assume.

All of humanity poured out its thoughts in reply. *Who are you? Why have you come?*

What do you want?

Suddenly a single voice broke through.

"Can I meet you?"

I knew that voice. It was Adamma!

We were astounded that a being that was f(
all intents and purposes the all-knowing God v
had imagined since the dawn of time would liste
to us all simultaneously and then choose to speak
one person.

"Yes, please do, child."

The being explained that he had been alone
long time and hoped that the intelligent life th
had evolved in this part of the galaxy would allo
him to share his experiences. The prospect
interstellar knowledge was intoxicating.

We learned that Old Abraham was reachir
out to our civilization in approximately a twent
light-year radius from the Darian moon. So I
wasn't God, but he was amazingly powerful.

And Old Earth was about twenty light yea
away.

Analysis of the news raced through Drago
Stead. People everywhere had heard the news firs
hand, so to speak, but they stopped what they we
doing to listen to the news feed and to think abo
where this would lead.

One place it led was to the end of war...
least for now.

Adamma asked if he would like to come
Erenarch, and suggested he serve on th
Foundation Board. There was some trepidation th
Erenarch would lose its authority, but O
Abraham said he would be honored ar
immediately put his technological expertise at th
disposal of the biological and AI people acro
Dragon Stead. The Norns were beside themselv

with happiness, although they continued to act like cranky old mothers. I thought the responsibility of looking after a bunch of illogical human creatures had taken a toll on them.

When news of Old Abraham's discovery broke, Andrew was in hospital recovering from wounds received in mopping up on Farana. Ashley hadn't heard he was back until Adamma told her about it.

"I don't know...," Ashley said, remembering the last fight she and Andrew had had.

"Oh, go on. At the very least you can thank him for that bracelet. I loaned him the credits to buy it, and it took him years to pay it off," Adamma said. Ashley was speechless.

Ashley went to visit Andrew, armed with with a bouquet of rosepithia flowers and a solemn expression. Her hair was back to its normal blonde, and she had temporarily removed most of her AI implants, except for a polished obsidian bracelet.

Ashley regarded him, floating in the medical field trussed up like a turkey. Suddenly she realized how much Andrew had done for her after Edward's death and how much he meant to her. She reached into the field and embraced him.

"Please forgive me," she said, burying her face on his shoulder. Those pesky tears were spilling from her eyes again. "I've been a fool."

"It's okay, Ashley. I've always loved you," Andrew replied, patting her gently on the back. "Now maybe you'd better get out of the medical field before you grow a new arm."

***

Old Abraham seemed to have taken a special shine to Adamma. As she grew up, her lineage of leadership blossomed along with her, thanks in r small part to Abraham's mentorship.

A few years after he joined the Erenarc Foundation, Adamma was invited to the Board, tl youngest ever to serve in that capacity.

The Faranan war had affected Adamma much as her fellow students, and she, Ashley, ar Andrew continued to be close friends. Togeth with Old Abraham, they worked to bring tl scourge of war to a halt across Dragon Stea (Adamma chaired the Foundation Board for ov twenty-five years, and I can see a bit of gray in h hair now. But she still has that innocent appearan that takes people off guard when they see h charge into the hairiest of diplomatic situations.

I've shepherded a whole generation students through Erenarch Academy, but I'm st proudest of my first class.)

With the latest conflict winding down, la year I entered my fifth decade at Erenarch ar thought of retiring soon. I still loved the kids ar seeing a new crop every year, but it had become little sadder for me each time they graduated ar moved on to higher-level positions within Erenarc I never married, but Erenarch became my famil Donal had said there was a place for me chairman of the literature department, but I to him I'd like to take the time to write some memoi and visit my mother on Tarant. I hadn't had chance to travel back there in decades.

Mom's place would be a great place to ki back and do some real writing in peace and quiet.

I was walking across the quadrangle or morning and saw Donal talking to a new teacher.

"Rowan!" he called. "Have you met the new maths teacher, George Richmond?" So this was the new blood. George seemed like a fine fellow, not nearly as much of a cold fish as Hilly.

"Rowan is going to retire next year," Donal said. "Unless we can get him to change his mind."

"I'd love to hear about your experiences, sir. I hear there's a daily teacher's meeting after work in the student union. Shall we see you there then?" George suggested.

"No need to call me sir," I replied, grinning. I could see we would spend many a happy hour hoisting flagons in the student union before I flew away.

The year sped by as I tried to tie up loose ends. Eventually I could see that loose ends inevitably just led to more unravelings. I came to realize that Erenarch Academy was now my home, even though I thought of Tarant most fondly. I made sure my students knew that it was about the closest planet to Heaven.

I went to Donal to retract my resignation, using the excuse that I hadn't really saved enough for retirement. He graciously accepted this ruse.

Donal threw a big reception for me, even though I wasn't retiring. The dragon banner holo waved gaily above the hall. The room was crowded with former and present students and faculty. Some must have spent months getting there.

Donal made a toast, saying, "We are fortunate indeed to have the Bard of Erenarch continue with us. His tales, songs, and poetry will remind us of the brave deeds and histories of our people and AIs for generations to come."

War's End and New Beginnings

I was touched to see the number of studen who traveled all the way back to Erenarch to so me. The most amazing sight was that the tir Declan had grown up to become a mighty warrio and poet in his own right.

"I'm highly indebted to you, Dr. C., n revered old rapscallion," he said, crushing my har in his huge grip. Still using the colorful vocabular I could see. I wouldn't be using a stylus for a whi until the bruising subsided a bit. He'd probab learned that handshake from Miranda.

Miranda didn't make it to the reunion. Aft the Faranan conflict, she moved back to Daris ar took a job as a military advisor. Her son Micha had recently graduated from Erenarch and kept n up to date. I heard she was involved in disarmament project on Daris.

One after another, my former students shoc my hand or hugged me. Adamma came up and p a rowan leaf garland around my head. "Now yc look like the real Green Man, Dr. C," she said.

"I'm glad you remember your mythologic references, young lady," I said, perhaps a little tc gruffly.

"Yes, well, at least we no longer have to reci epics word for word these days," she retorted wi a smile.

And Rick. He had become an ecologic expert and had been working on the reclamation Anberra.

My current students hung back a while ar then crowded in for hugs.

I felt a tingling at the base of my skull, ar Old Abraham made his presence known.

"Congratulations, Dr. Creeve. I'm really enjoying this celebration. It is wonderful to see all of this good will. Your students—and Adamma in particular—certainly have strong affection for you, although they don't often make a show of it."

"Thanks, Abraham. You know, sometimes I'm glad I can't read minds like you. I'd probably go around crazy half the time."

"No more so than I do," Abraham replied. "In fact, right now, I'm a bit concerned about some thoughts I've heard originating on Overman Prime. It's reassuring that you and the Norns are staying on. I think we're going to need you. If you'll pardon me, I need to talk with Doctors Gray and Gerhart."

Overman Prime? No human had yet ventured as far as the Overman star system. But with Abe's help, maybe we could once again spit in the face of the universe.

In spite of the bittersweet partings and hints of more bedlam to come, this was an exciting, golden time for Dragon Stead's civilizations. I felt grateful to have learned as much from my friends and students as I taught them. They continued to show me the way, and I didn't want to miss a minute of their future.

Fare thee well, my children, and don't forget to write.

And I'll continue to do the same.

*****~~~~~*****

About the Author

Juliana Rew is a software engineer and former science and technical writer for the National Center for Atmospheric Research (NCAR). She has won more than a dozen technical writing competitions. She mentored minority and female college science interns in writing scientific papers. She advocates digital preservation of literary works and has produced several public domain books for Project Gutenberg. Her blog is The Well-Rounded Geek (http://thewell-roundedgeek.blogspot.com), and you can peruse her other fiction forays at her author website, julianarew.com.

Art Credits

Cover: Keely Rew

*****~~~~~*****

Discover other titles by Juliana Rew:

Miranda of Daris
Mountain Ma'am
The Adventures of Mountain Ma'am

www.julianarew.com